A RATHER BORING BOOK

THE MIDDLE CHILD OF BOOKS, ONE MIGHT EVEN SAY

L. H. DRAKEN

GRAUBÄR PRESS

Copyright © 2020 by L. H. Draken

All rights reserved.

~2nd edition~

All characters and names in this book have been fictionalized. Any resemblance of characters herein and real people is usually coincidental. But sometimes not. Sometimes the guilty are left to burn in the glorious shame of their true identity — you know who you are.

No part of this book may be reproduced in any form or by any electronic or mechanical means, including information storage and retrieval systems, without written permission from the author, except for the use of brief quotations in a book review.

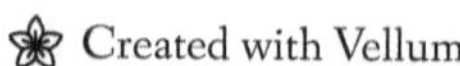 Created with Vellum

For Robert Reidy,

on the occasion of his thirtieth birthday.

— September 22, 2020 —

The tradition of giving books, as well intentioned as it is, needs changing. This book hopes to be one step forward in that process. Or, perhaps at least a single alternative to help a gift-giving-bro out.

When an avid reader gives a friend an adored book, they gift not just an object but an obligation. Not only does the gift imply that they expect the receiver to read the book, but to appreciate it as much as they themselves have[1]. This, more often than not, negates the very good will which was intended by the gift. Gifts should not be obligations.

We've all seen the Instagram stories of how Norwegians (or some other snobby nordic people) have the tradition of gifting books for Christmas. People receive the books, then retreat to their rooms and spend the rest of the night reading, like the happy introverts such a custom implies. Invariably, these social media shares accompany the post with comments like "why don't we all do this??" And "I wish we were all Norwegian!"

No you don't! Maybe someone gives you a great book

and you start it that night — but how many perfectly delightful books end up stacked up year on year? Let people choose their own books! Books are no longer limited by financial means — you're not doing something for people they can't do for themselves — that's the freedom the lending library gave us. More often than not, they're actually cheap gifts. *The written word is not the financial flex it used to be.*

But I'm no utopian idealist. People will continue to give books as gifts, and because most of the time it's done from a place of good will, I'll not be sore about it. I have myself received many great books which I've read and have gained great pleasure from.

But—

— but I'd like to let us ameliorate the weight of guilt incumbent on such gifts. That's what this book is for. The book you hold in your hands allows the you the literary satisfaction of continuing the great tradition of giving story to your friend — while not burdening the receiver with the Irish-Catholic level guilt connected with probably never reading the book. This book is the opposite of 'my favorite book ever'. This book is forthcoming with its value. It's fairly boring. It needn't be read. You needn't feel obligated to forgo your favorite Netflix show in order to read it and come back to the giver with your stumbled-over and wholly fatuous literary praise. It's okay! There's nothing much to say about this book, besides that it saves you much of the boring bits of a full novel and when there is text, keeps it short and simple.

.

.

.

1. This practice is even worse than watching a favorite TV show with a girlfriend/boyfriend, which is itself a minefield of potential sorrow and disappointment. In that situation the significant other feels the extra weight of appreciating and enjoying the show just as much as the introducer does, and when they fail to laugh at the same points or cry at the appropriate scenes as their beloved, both parties often feel the disappointment of not sharing 'this too'. Or worse, 'do we even get each other'? But gifting a book is an even *higher* time commitment and demand for attention.

I don't want you to think you're just giving someone a bunch of blank pages. Granted — that would be *the most* boring book. But there is some intellectual nourishment yet to be had. I'll just do you the favor of cutting out some of the potatoes and giving you more of the meat. To that end, within these pages there are a subset of the elements necessary to all great archetypal stories.

For instance — in every comedy story, there's a 'the friends meet', or as writer types put it, there's a 'meet-cute'. This book has that scene. Then there are often, mixed in with the drama and character development some highlightable 'quotable quotes'. Great lines that make you laugh or think twice or otherwise bear repeating. I'll give you those without the fluff of all the other stuff and put the good lines out there in the open. In the tradition of Dostoevsky, there is an essay mixed into the middle of a story. His usually pertain directly to the story, but since the story here is quite brief, don't beat yourself up if you don't follow from what part of the plot the essay necessitates.

A horror story always has a 'Hero at the mercy of the

villain' — think *Daniel Craig strapped in a dentist chair and a drill aimed directly at his temple.* A cheap airport-bookstore bodice-ripper has, well, a bodice-ripping scene. We'll keep it PG-13, but, you'll know it when you see it. Consider this fair warning.

Some characters will pop up where you least expect them, maybe there will be an illustration or two, there might be a bit of an inside joke between the reader and his audience — don't worry if you don't get it. You're not supposed to. Near the end there will be the open question that makes you wonder what will possibly happen next, *in the sequel.* We got you covered—gotta keep you connected as a reading fan, right?

"ALL THIS HAPPENED, MORE OR LESS."
— Kurt Vonnegut, Slaughterhouse Five

CHAPTER 1

It was a dark and stormy night. ...

... Lightning flashed and thunder crashed, covering Janet's cries for help. No one would rescue her. No one could even hear her. The knife in the back of her shoulder throbbed, but she dared not touch it. She collapsed on her side, her head diagonal to the step, Madam Bavaria staring down at her from her stone pedestal. Who would have thought Oktoberfest could go so terribly wrong. Even in the one year it was canceled. (THRILLER)

... Una sat in the deep window seat of her grandmothers old farmhouse-turned-country-inn, staring out at the dilapidated stone out-buildings and ancient farm equipment. How would her true love ever find her out here, in the middle of nowhere? (ROMANCE)

. . .

... James Roy swung up on his horse, chaps soaked, hat funneling a stream of water off the brim of his ten gallon hat and down his back. His horse was plum tuckered out, and if the light in the window of the one-room farmstead up ahead wasn't friendly, he might just die of exposure. A long swill of strong whiskey was what he needed. (WESTERN)

... Fewer people than usual would show up for this evenings "Snobby Classics" Book club. Robert had been at it long enough to know weather had a significant impact on attendance. Which was fine. He tried to stay laid back about that sort of thing.

He'd come late to reading the classics. Indeed, this was exactly why he'd started the club — to read the books he felt guilty about not already having read. And to meet similar sorts of people with whom to complain about them. Not that he was a nerd. If anything he'd been a jock in school. But as he got older, and he'd soon be thirty, his adult-self was turning into something of a whiskey sipping, classics reading, sweater wearing, country gentleman sort. (LITERARY FICTION)

The point is, you can start with the same first line, and head very different, immediately recognizable, directions. So you better know what sort of story you're in. As Jung said, (paraphrase), you're all living a story, but if you don't know what story it is, you might not be playing the lead role in your own drama—you might not even like the role you're playing.

CHAPTER 2

GREAT BOOKS usually have a few great lines. Something that makes you think, or makes you laugh, or wisdom that will stay with you after you've forgotten what the story was about. The good ones find a way to mix some of those things together — wit with wisdom, sadness with a laugh.

For the sake of saving you time, I've gone to the trouble of removing all the window dressing around some of the best lines. Here, for instance, is a great line from Slaughterhouse five—

.

.

"...When a Tralfamadorian sees a corpse, all he thinks is that the dead person is in a bad condition in that particular moment, but that the same person is just fine in plenty of other moments. Now, when I myself hear that somebody is dead, I simply shrug and say what the Tralfamadorians say, ...which is 'So it goes.'"

—Kurt Vonnegut

.

.

.

Often great lines are mixed in around boring bits. Shoe leather, some people say. It has to be there, to get you to the next event but it's not any fun. I'll just cut out the in-between and get you straight to the good stuff.

.

.

.

<<...boring bits excised>>

.

.

.

.

.

.

.

.

.

.

.

.

.

.

.

.

.

.

.

.

.

.

"It's a lot like Vonnegut's own war experience," Joe said slowly in his usual 'cowboy on the range' methodical way, "but not—". It sounded like he was confused, but people who knew him knew it was just his way of getting into an idea. Joe was deliberate in everything he did. He wasn't a man for quick wit, but once on a problem he didn't let go till he had a solution. And he always came to the solution. It was his lawyer type brain.

"I think that's just the point," Katherine jumped in, as if she'd already been thinking about it. "The book is probably exactly his experience. I'd even bet he knew a psycho like Roland Weary. That's where these sorts of stories come from — you can hardly make them up. But the ways it's different are intentional. They're different to serve a specific purpose. Like Valencia, the really fat woman he marries after the war. That's not Vonnegut's wife in real life. But he's changing the character to make an analogy to the way he feels Americans came back from the war: instead of changing anything meaningful after the carnage they saw, they settled in for the comfortable life, unable to talk about the hard stuff. She's fat and ugly and not very smart and they don't have any real conversations, but she has money. And her dad sets him up with the ophthalmology practice. Billy Pilgrim makes the compromise to marry her so he can have the easier life. And then there is his job as an ophthalmologist—"

"Yeah, what does that mean?" Robert asked. "Why change that. Why not just leave Billy Pilgrim a writer? It would make sense, style wise. That he's telling his experience, and writing it as an autobiography—"

"*Because*—" Katherine drew the word out slowly, one corner of her mouth twisting in a smile, one eyebrow raised as if being pushed up by the smirk, "As an Ophthalmologist, his job is to help people see clearly. *And yet* he's completely blind."

Robert looked at her for a moment, eyes slightly narrowed, then he pinched his thumb and forefinger in an "A-okay" gesture, and raised the fingers to his lips, taking a long drag on an invisible joint.

"Duuuude," he said, his chest puffed out, holding the imaginary-doped air in his lungs as long as he could to preserve the high, "stoner moment!" He choked and let the rest of the air drain from his chest in an exaggerated slow blow out and laughed.

Katherine threw back her head in satisfaction and mirrored his laughter. This was the first time she'd made it to a "Snobby Books" discussion. She'd sat down at the table and laid her neon-green backpack and helmet on the bench next to her only an hour earlier. "oh, *you're* Katherine," Robert, had said as soon as she'd introduced herself. She'd already hosted one of his meetings—a second discussion for Pride and Prejudice—but they'd never met in person. "We finally speak in the flesh," he said in his charming Irish accent.

He was immediately likable. The sort of person everyone could get on with.

.

.

.

'... so it goes.' — *Kurt Vonnegut*

CHAPTER 3

.

.

.

.

.

.

.

.

<<character background / boring bits>>

.

.

.

.

.

.

.

"It's enough for me to be sure that you and I exist at this
moment."
— Gabriel García Márquez,
One Hundred Years of Solitude

.

.

.

.

.

.

.

<<character background / boring bits>>

.

.

.

.

.

.

.

.

.

.

.

At Christmas-time they met at the medieval Christmas market for mulled wine and roasted almonds. The square was packed with people and they had to wriggle through the masses like earthworms in packed earth to get mugs of mulled wine and food. But they stayed in the middle of the crowd in the surprisingly warm evening despite the jostling. He talked about the ranch at home—his brother and dad and about things he used to do as a boy growing up in the Wild West—and she made fun of him for living a cliche.

"Did you have your own pony, and use a slingshot on prairie dogs and squirrels?"

"No!" He said in mock insult. "I mean, I might have had a slingshot," he smirked, "but we used a gun on prairie dogs.

Those suckers carry the bubonic plague and their holes can break a cows leg."

She laughed, "Of course you had a gun. What, for your 8th birthday?"

"6th."

She shook her head and grinned.

"It's funny. I never felt like much of a rancher when I was there. My dad and brother have it in their blood - dust and cow shit buried so deep in the crevices of their skin they'll never be clean. My brother always made me feel like I wasn't much of a man. Even when we were both kids I knew I would never be a rancher like him. I tried, for a while, but it wasn't in my bones like it was for my dad and him. So eventually I stopped trying to copy him in being a rancher and found things I actually liked. It's when I started really reading a lot and writing."

"So you left and came out here."

"Yes ma'am. Left the ranch to live the big city life. Ironically, it wasn't till I showed up in New York that I felt like a rancher for the first time in my life."

She talked about going to Long Island with a girlfriend. She didn't have enough vacation saved to go all the way back to California for Christmas so had made plans to stay with her friend's family. "It's not the same though,' she said. They're super nice, but it's different. You notice it most at Christmas when you're supposed to be home.'

They started with small mugs of hot chocolate with whipped cream melting on top, but then took turns buying rounds of overpriced mulled wine. As the hot sugar and alcohol warmed them, they made a couple rounds with schnapps added to the hot wine. The crowds thinned, but neither one was ready to call it a night and go home. They stuck around at the edges of the party, more interested in talking than the live music playing or the booths selling knit things and medieval-style jewelry. Eventually it was just them in the square, standing near the statue and a few hangers-on.

"I have a present for you," she finally said, pulling her bag off her shoulder.

"Aw shit," he sighed. "Not really?"

"Of course!"

"But I didn't get you anything."

"You didn't need to. But you were so helpful in our creative writing class when I was having a hard time. It's as much a thank you as anything. It just happens to also be Christmas now that our class is done."

"Damn," He let out a heavy sigh of almost-annoyance. "You're going to make me stand here and open a present like a fool while I have nothing to give you in return. Do you intentionally think of ways to punish your friends, or does it just come naturally?"

She grinned in completely un-masked glee. "It comes naturally!" She was almost giddy with excitement for having out-gifted him, or about the present he hadn't yet opened, he wasn't sure. He couldn't help but be pleased with her infectious smile.

"Come over here where there's more room," she pulled him by the arm to the side of the square. He saw a bench on the opposite side of the street and suggested they go over there, "where there is at least the illusion of privacy."

They crossed and sat down, he in the middle, she right next to him. It had gotten colder, as the night grew late. Or their circulation was failing them as five glasses of hot spiced wine and schnapps made it through their system and depressed their circulation. She huddled close to him on the bench.

He sighed, trying to act annoyed at having to open a present, but it was a flat imitation of irritation. He was more than a little pleased she had thought of him and her childish glee about the present was infectious.

"I had such a trouble getting this! It's just a silly little thing. I got an advert for it on my phone during Black Friday. I thought of you and immediately bought it. But then I filled in the address one letter wrong, so it never arrived. I had to email the company, and track it down, and eventually they said they'd send a new one, but this was already last week, so I went downtown to buy the thing again at their pop-up store. Of course they didn't have it in stock anymore, so I had to get something else. But—" She gave a long, exaggerated sigh, the details of her story washing over him without really registering into memory.

He grinned as he opened the wrapping. "Notebooks. Of course." His grin turned into a laugh.

"Leather-bound. Plain black. Unlined. After my new-apartment warming party, and the ridiculous discussion about how real books are written by hand and everything. When I saw the sale I just couldn't resist."

He carefully laid the set of three notebooks back in the box, and put the lid back on, turning it over in his hands.

She put her head on his shoulder, one arm now threaded around his elbow and wrapped up around his bicep like the snake on the healing scepter of asclepius. He could feel the soft rise and fall of her breathing even through her wool coat, the back of his arm tight against her chest. The alcohol was thick in his head. He couldn't see or sense anything but the shape of the woman next to him. The world around him was a still life and only she was alive.

He looked down at the top of her head, tilted just slightly back so her face looked barely toward the night sky. She'd closed her eyes, her face no longer the mirthful laugh of a few moments earlier, but relaxed and happy. He leant his head down, touching his mouth to the top of her head. He didn't dare kiss her, but breathed in the sent of her hair. She tightened her hold on his arm, pulled it even closer against her body. Before he could question what he was doing, he'd taken his free hand and reached around to her chin and lifted her face up to his.

She didn't open her eyes, didn't resist.

He brought his face to hers, the tip of his nose to hers, his lips to hers.

She tasted of red wine and cinnamon.

He unwrapped his arm from her, and slid it behind her, finding her waist and holding her tight against him. She kissed him back, as if her body were melting into him, whipped cream on hot chocolate.

CHAPTER 4

IN A ROMANCE you'd go from the 'boy meets girl' to a bit of background and story development.

But some stories are *only* development. They're just pages and pages of exposition and description with no actual plot to speak of. Surprisingly, they still sometimes make it into the canon of 'Great Literature'.

I've no idea why.

In literary fiction, these bits are sometimes written so beautifully you don't even realize nothing's happening. Or you notice but don't give a flying fridge, because you're enjoying yourself anyway. Or these stories might have unique new themes that haven't been written about before, so people allow plot to be absence because the description is so imaginative. But the fact remains, they've no real story. No real drama. Nothing to really get hooked on.

These stories go from one description of a scene to the next, one description of a character to the next, and every complication that might possibly lead to real drama or plot development is magically resolved before anything messy happens.

I'd never be so snitchy as to label these books by name —
but in the spirit of saving you the trouble of reading them,
but still represent them in this meta-book, the rest of this
chapter is excised for your convenience. You're welcome.

.

.

.

.

.

.

.

.

.

.

.

.

.

.

.

.

Captain Nemo replied coldly, "The earth does not need
new continents, it needs new men."
Twenty-thousand Leagues under the Sea —Jules Verne

.

.

.

.

.

    .

"To renounce that unendurable worldly yoke which men believe to be liberty is not perhaps so painful as you think."

Twenty-thousand Leagues under the Sea —Jules Verne

<<and on it goes>>

.

.

.

.

To BE fair to the spectrum of story, not all books have just one plot. Some are a mix of micro stories — each with their own rises and falls and resolutions. If a set of short stories is put together well, it will be both the individual stories but also show an overarching development and meta story. But despite all this discussion of plot and crisis, some writers really buck the desire for plot and focus on character and individual internal development. We call these boring books 'Literary Fiction'.

.

.

.

.

.

.

.

.

.

.

'...her name was like a summons to all my foolish blood. Her image accompanied me even in places the most hostile to romance....

'...at night... her image came between me and the page I strove to read.' —*Araby, Dubliners*

'He gnawed the rectitude of his life; he felt that he had been outcast from life's feast. One person had seemed to love him and he had denied her life and happiness...' *A Painful Case, Dubliners*

.

.

.

Compilers note:

Something I've come to realize as I read more broadly, is that there are very few 'enduring love' stories. Romance is a theme layered in with many genres of story, but almost always it is the 'lovers meet' story. Rarely do you read a good 'love enduring' story — the epic of a full relationship— of what love becomes over the journey of a life together. Is this so rare an occurrence we don't know how to write it? Is it because everyone can fall in love, but so few can remain there, that we don't have very much to say about it?

.

.

.

.

.

.

.

.

.

.

.

..

.

.

.

.

.

.

.

.

.

.

.

.

.

'A wave of yet more tender joy escaped from his heart and went coursing in warm blood along his arteries. Like the tender fire of stars moments of their life together, that no one knew of or would ever know of, broke upon and illumined his memory. ... For the years, he felt, had not quenched his soul or hers.'
—*The Dead, Dubliners*

.

.

.

'He did not like to say even to himself that her face was no longer beautiful, but he knew that it was no longer the face for which Michael Furey had braved death.'
—*The Dead, Dubliners*

.

.

.

.

.

.

.

.

<<Boring Bits>>

<<Boring Bits>>

.

.

.

.

.

.

.

.

.

.

.

\<\<Boring Bits\>\>

.

.

.

.

.

.

.

.

.

.

.

.

.

.

.

. / L. H. DRAKEN

.

.

.

.

.

<<Boring Bits>>

.

.

<<Boring Bits>>

.

.

.

.

.

.

.

.

.

.

.

.

.

.

.

.

.

.

.

.

.

.

.

<<Boring Bits>>

.

.

.

.

.

.

.

.

.

.

.

.

.

.

.

.

.

.

.

.

.

.

.

<<Boring Bits>>

.

.

/ L. H. DRAKEN

.

.

.

.

.

.

.

.

.

.

.

.

.

<<Boring Bits>>

.

.

.

.

.

.

.

.

.

.

.

.

.

.

.

.

.

.

.

.

.

.

.

.

.

.

.

.

.

.

.

.

.

.

.

.

.

.

.

.

32 / L. H. DRAKEN

.

.

James Joyce

IF YOU READ one author long enough, you'll find they often have a favorite thing to turn into metaphor. I've found, for instance, Graham Greene has a brilliant way of describing alcohol. It's in his books like it's own character, playing its own role, sometimes behind the scenes like a fairy godmother, sometimes terribly front and center like a bad court jester.

"He held a small spot of brandy in his glass warily - as if it was an animal to which he gave shelter, but not trust."
— *The Power and the Glory, Graham Greene*

.

.

.

"The glass of chocolate liqueur might have been a crystal, the way he looked at it and turned it this way and that."
— *The Third Man, Graham Greene*

.

.

.

.

.

.

.

.

.

.

.

.

.

.

.

.

.

One starts to realize that the more you read a certain author, the more their view of the world—their idiosyncrasies and oddities and their relationship to the physical—will be revealed in their work, whether or not intentional. Even down to the way they describe such every day objects as a tumbler full of whiskey.

CHAPTER 7

Ah. We've come so far.

For people who study story, say specifically crime and thrillers, there is general consensus that there are three major parts of a thriller. The beginning hook, where we meet the hero and the insighting crime, the middle build, where the plot thickens and we learn about the villain, and the crisis and resolution where the hero wins and the villain is destroyed.

Here we are, in the middle build, where the villain shines. Here we learn the mind of evil, the thoughts and motivation and power which our hero is up against. The dark and powerful forces which our hero cannot possibly overcome.

.

.

.

.

.

.

.

.

.

.

.

.

.

.

.

.

.

.

.

.

.

.

.

.

.

.

\<boring bits of middle build\>

.

.

. / L. H. DRAKEN

.

.

.

.

.

<inside the villains mind>

'I am the spirit that denies forever!
And rightly so! What has arisen from the void deserves
to be annihilated.
It would be best if nothing ever would arise.
And thus what you call havoc,
Deadly sin, or briefly stated: Evil,
That is my proper element.

...I am a portion of that part which once was everything.'
—*Faust*, Goethe

*As far as thriller-story structure, this is often where we
finally name the villain and see inside his mind or world.*

.

.

.

.

.

.

Vladimir's focus fell on a perfectly white pigeon pecking at crumbs on the rim of a stone fountain near his park bench. The pure feathers of the pigeon's coat looked like lace fringing a baptismal gown. Vladimir closed his eyes and tried to focus again on his problem.

"You have to hide it for me!" A little girl interrupted him, her doll-like voice piercing through his scattered thoughts. He opened his eyes and saw a child standing before him, bouncy curls glowing white-blonde in the sun, holding out a fifty-cent euro-piece in her pudgy palm. He closed his eyes, hoping she'd disappear like an apparition if he simply didn't interact with it. The child repeated her demand. For some inexplicable reason, she'd picked him of all the strangers in the park to play 'treasure hunt' with. Vladimir grudgingly opened his eyes and took the coin from her hand and palmed it. The dark sunglasses, set jaw, and scowl, his usual tools for discouraging contact with strangers, had been ineffectual with the girl-child. He predicted she'd develop a liking for problem boys in her teenage years.

He let the coin slip from his fingers and rest on the seat where he'd been sitting.

"Hide it!" The child told him for the third time.

He rose slowly from the bench.

"Close your eyes," he commanded, not even trying to soften his voice. She clapped one pudgy hand over her eyes, fingers splayed wide enough to see clearly through. He didn't address the transgression of the rules of play. It seemed a bit Toni-Soprano of him to complain about her not following the rules of her own game. Just like his Italian mobster-hero, he demanded high adherence to the agreed laws of interaction, but he struggled to always adhere to his own principles. If anything he was mostly annoyed that she thought he was fool enough to not realize she was cheating.

The late twenty-something man stood and walked over to the small fountain facing his park bench, right fist closed tight as if it still hid the coin. He glanced over his shoulder like a dime-store hero trying to escape a tail. He knew he wouldn't escape his pursuer, but wanted to see if she'd turned to watch him. She had. Even if she'd hidden her eyes better, her excited grin gave away her corrupt intentions. She'd even moved a step or two forward, not satisfied to wait till he'd told her his task was done. The child was practically pawing the ground to prove she could outsmart him. Kids! They make up these games and then didn't even play by their own rules. The fact that he was alive was proof enough he wasn't so easily played.

He slipped his empty fist in the the water at edge of the shallow fountain and pretended to touch the slimy bottom, dropping a nonexistent coin, then brought his empty hand back up, fingers spread wide proving he no longer held the treasure. Having not closed her eyes even to blink, she needed no verbal command to tell her the coin was hidden and she could begin her search. She flung her hand aside and bounded the last remaining steps to the fountain.

The deception kids learn in so little time, he thought. She couldn't be older than five, and already she'd gone from suckling infant not knowing mother from monkey to flaxen-haired trickster, ready to lie, cheat, and steal her way to success.

The girl, delighted by the chance to display her superior detective skills, practically dove into the fountain where he'd faked the drop, plunging both arms shoulder-deep in the water, wetting the tiny sleeves of her perfectly white sundress as she raked the bottom of the pool, determined to retrieve her treasure. Vladimir doubted the frilly layers would be white much longer.

The villain-turned-treasure-hider turned, not even pretending to conceal a grin as he went back to his bench. He picked up the boring medical-mystery novel he'd been pretending to read and resumed his place in the shade. Vladimir glanced down at the space next to him, picked up the coin, and held it in his free hand, playing with it between his fingers. When the girl returned to demand how he'd made it vanish so completely, she'd notice it directly.

He spent one more glance on the girl before he closed his eyes and returned his mental energy to the problem he'd been stuck on before her interruption. He'd written the phishing email himself, had built the landing page to perfectly mimic the expected login screen. He'd engineered the virus to seamlessly insert itself into the network and lock down the system for his access alone.

The problem was, he didn't know how to eject.

Getting in was his specialty. But for this particular system, he couldn't seem to hack in without leaving a trail straight back to himself. What good was all the bitcoin in the world if Eastern-European thugs were going to rip your porcelain-white programmers' body to shreds the next morning?

Vladimir tried again to focus his chi, but instead the little girl's curly-white hair blocked his vision until he was brought back to the scene before him. As he watched, astounded, the feminine trickster, obviously unable to find the coin, reached one stealthy hand down to the pocket of her lace-fringed sundress, then, fist clenched around some new treasure, swiped her hand through the water, shrieking with joy as she brought her hand up and announced to all within earshot her success at finding the coin.

"The little—" he whispered to himself as she trotted back to him, arms still soaked in scummy fountain water, the front of her dress now sporting a new mossy-green smear, a grin larger than her mouth smeared across her whole face. To say she was proud of her hunting prowess was a gross understatement. A gold twenty-cent piece shone in her outstretched palm.

'You little scheister!' he said, not sure if he were impressed or annoyed that she'd cheated him out of his planned moment of triumph.

Then a thought hit him. The girl faded from sight, only her Cheshire-Cat grin lingering in his vision slightly longer than the rest of her form. The original fifty-cent piece fell from his fingers as the solution to his problem struck him like a pile of golden coins falling from the sky. Of course!

The girl-child, having entirely evaporated, impeded him nothing in his rush to exit the garden, but he nearly tackled a balding, middle-aged man feeding ducks at the other end of the fountain. The man was only barely able to step aside before Vladimir careened past him out of the park. The necessity to get to his keyboard before the solution the female-devil had unwittingly played out to his problem was overwhelming. It possessed him like a spirit, driving him to implement the solution to his work. He had to incorporate the wisdom the spirit had gifted him before the dream left him and presented itself to someone else.

A perfectly white pigeon, disturbed by the sudden rush of movement as the Serbian fled the park, fluttered into the air and settled on the vacated bench and returned to preening it's lacey-white feathers.

CHAPTER 8

SCENE: *Basement of a dive bar in a disreputable corner of a Dublin ghetto. Windows are coated in a layer of soot that looks like it must have been accumulating since the early days of the industrial revolution. A barkeep polishes glasses with a gray rag as he removes them from the drawer of a dish-washer below the counter. He has the expert-level barkeep skill of seeming to pay no attention at all to anyone but not missing even a single playfully-bit lower-lip.*

A man at the far end of the counter, huddled neatly against the wall, protects the dregs of a Guinness he's been mothering like a helicopter-parent since well before either of our two leads walked in. Otherwise the bar is empty.

Two street-hardened gangsters sit at a battered table, sipping two whiskey neats from two chipped glass tumblers. The sorry excuse for a table is close enough to call directly to the barkeeper for refills but far enough to retain the privacy of their conversation.

The larger of the gangsters has his forearms flat on the table, shoulders square, biceps flexed. The smaller of the two is leaning back in her chair, palms flat on the table in front of her, but making a good show of not being intimidated by his alpha-male posturing.

SHE : We're something of a pair, you and I—

HE : *Drags on cigarette, his tattooed knuckles spelling out half a word. He takes his time blowing out the smoke slowly, then—*
You think so, punk? Because I hear I'm rubber and you're glue--

SHE : Luck sticks to me and bounces off you?
The broad raises her glass to a one-sided toast of her wit.

In one swift motion, he pulls a switch blade from his back pocket, snaps it open, and jams the blade into the table between the open fingers of her hand.

HE : So that's how it is? Well you're not invited to my birthday party anymore.

SHE : *Runs one elegant finger up the sharp edge of the blade,*
Too bad. The toast I wrote was even better than last year.

She shrugs her shoulders and downs the last of her whiskey, then raises the empty to the barman who, like all barkeeps, hasn't missed a single one of their movements, being as they're both exactly what a barkeep recognizes is trouble ready to ignite.

SHE : We'll be needing two more of these.

HE : *Turns to barman,*
Make it the Bushmills. This one knows her shit.
Turns back to the broad, and for just a moment drops out of character,
Wait. Do you know how to shoot a game of pool?

SHE : I do.
She raises one eyebrow in skepticism,
Why—?

** Director stands up from her deck chair, turns to the hotty with the script next to her** "Wait. We have to ask if the dame can shoot a game of pool but in this scene the dude all of a sudden has tattooed knuckles? No one asked if *that* was consistent ?!?"
Drops back into chair, waves to camera man, "Carry on—"

** Scene continues**

The two gangsters move to the pool tables and play round after round on the thread-worn upholstered table, dropping ball after ball in the pockets, neither showing a clear advantage over the other.

Hours pass.

No one else but the barkeep is in the bar, the helecopter-drunk having finally stumbled out the door. Empty whiskey glasses line one edge of the greencarpeted table.

TAT-KNUCKLES : Black, left corner pocket

She leans on her cue, one hip thrust to the side, and gives him a mocking smile that makes it clear she doubts his aim. Then she bites her bottom lip.

His cue catches the table, rips into the already thinned green carpet. Black remains untouched, glasses shatter.

The Barkeep, who has been watching every shot from his post on the other side of the room, bursts into laughter.

BARKEEP : What the hell happened??

TAT-KNUCKLES : She... it was the... *throws cue on ground.*
  Aw nevermind!

The dame throws a scowl at the barkeep who quickly turns back to polishing the dry class in his hand.

DAME : Oh, you missed the shot? Sorry. I was... watching

something else... while you were bent over, lining up to *miss.*

Tat-knuckles : Listen toots. You need to behave while I'm holding the wood. You'll get your turn soon enough.

** Network executives walk in*
"Look guys... Either you throw out the schoolyard insults or you drop the soft-core porn in the next act. WE CAN'T MARKET THIS!"

The dame straightens up from where she'd been preparing to school tat-knuckles with a winning shot. "So you're saying... make it harder porn? I mean, I can shift gears. But I think this one," **throws a thumb over her shoulder** "is still sore about being unlucky rubber."

Dame turns back to Tat-Knuckles, with his weathered Irish charm and easy-distractability. "what'cha gonna bring, mister? Think you've got it in you to make this show worth their money?"

Tat-Knuckles to fellow C-List acting companion, "Love, you're talking to the Dublin Under-Ten, basketball vice-captain, 1997-1999. I've handled pressure you can't even imagine.

Network execs reappear "C'mon guys. Comedy or porn? Make up your minds!"

Tat-Knuckles and Dame in unison : "Both"
No-look high-five.

A Russian Post-Production guy runs in from right stage, "AAALLLL WRONG!! The lighting is ALLL WRONG!"

Director rolls her eyes and gestures for the scene to continue, ignoring Russian.

Tat-Knuckles shouts over to makeup "I need a touchup on the tear-drop tattoo. I splashed some apple juice when I broke the 'whiskey' glasses.

Ditzy makeup girl rushes over to attend his needs.

** Scene Continues **

Dame turns back to Tat-Knuckles, cue stick still resting on the floor like her trident. She takes a step forward, one foot now level between both of his, and leans in close enough to smell the apple juice on his breath, then tilts sideways and whispers in his ear, lips nearly brushing his skin—

DAME: "I think we both know *I'll* handle the pressure just fine"

**director in deck chair waves frantically at the camera guy, hissing* "make sure to get the Russian out of the shot!"

Dame moves back, bends over and drops the last of her striped balls into a middle pocket.

. . .

Tat-Knuckles : You know your way around the wood pretty well. Think you could handle something, more substantial?

Writer sweating and flicking madly through script "Oh god. They're going improv!?"

Dame straightens up and takes a step back to face Tat-Knuckles face-to-face.
Dame : I've seen your aim. You sure you can make the shot?

Network execs throw up their hands in utter frustration and storm off set. One waves his PA over as he exits, "call the X-rated films people - maybe they can do something with this"

PA nods but turns back as soon as the exec is out of the room to finish watching the scene.

Scene continues

Tat-Knuckles grabs her by both hips and pulls her against him. She drops her cue and pushes both hands flat against his chest, limiting how close he gets.
Tat-Knuckles : *turns to barkeep,* "Hey Jack, I'll lock up tonight."

Barkeep : Sure thing, Tat-Knuckles.
Barkeep disappears off stage left.

· · ·

TAT-KNUCKLES : *turning back to dame. 'I'll make the shot.'*
Dame narrows her eyes, then undoes the top button of his jean shirt.

TAT-KNUCKLES : You rip my shirt and I'll take you right here.

The Dame's fingers stop for a moment, then in one movement she grabs both sides of his button-down and rips it open. Buttons fly across the dirty bar floor like M&M's from a bag of ripped candies.

Tat-Knuckles lifts the feather-weight gangster up and sets her on the rim of the pool table.

SCENE[1]

---

1. See what I did there? I know only one other book where the author drops in one random scene from the script of a play after about 500 pages of normal prose-fiction.
   Now we know two books.
   —and we went meta.

CHAPTER 9

.

.

.

.

.

.

<boring details of the *middle build*>

.

.

.

.

.

.

.

.

.

.

.

.

<boring bits>

Joyce is known for having no plot. But he sure does know his way around a dictionary and poetic pros!

"The sea, the snotgreen sea, the scrotumtightening sea."

.

.

.

.

.

.

.

.

.

.

"He foresaw his pale body reclined in it at full, naked, in a womb of warmth, ... his navel, bud of flesh; and saw the dark tangled curls of his bush floating, floating hair of the stream around the limp father of thousands, a languid floating flower."

.

.

.

.

.

.

.

.

.

.

.

.

.

<boring bits>

.

.

58 / L. H. DRAKEN

.

.

.

— James Joyce, Ulysses

.

.

.

.

.

.

.

.

.

.

.

.

.

.

.

.

You're welcome. You've no idea what a service I just did you. What amounts of time you saved having those extra bits cut out. Now you can use those moments to do other more worthy things... like washing your goldfish or de-dandelioning your lawn, or counting the toothpicks on the diner table, or ...

CHAPTER 10

READ enough classics and you start to appreciate the retro-spective humor of archaic speech. Because—damn. They said a lot of illicit things and no one seemed to mind. Mostly, I suppose, because when they said them it wasn't illicit — it's just the adjustments of time to our diction that has changed the double-entendre of phrases to no longer be purely superficial. I take that back. I think there have always been DE's, and writers just got away with making those jokes because the prudes that would take offense weren't aware.

Even the dear and completely clean Dame Agatha Christie falls pray to the ravages (*cough) of time's illicit battle with the entropy of respectability. One of her most beloved characters says the most *inappropriate* things! Telling old spinsters to 'make a *clean breast* of things'. Mmmhmm. Or like a true pedophile, he'll tell young girls to, and I quote,

'See now, mademoiselle,' he said very gently, 'it is Papa Poirot who asks you this. The old Papa Poirot who has much knowledge and much experience. I would not seek to entrap you, <<*cough* *sure* *cough*>> mademoiselle. Will you not trust me and tell me ...?'

Papa Poirot??? Tell me the theme music for a B-list basement-mutilation scene isn't playing in the back of your head when you read that.

.

.

.

But he uses that phrase over and over again, across different novels!

"What one does not tell Papa Poirot, he finds out."

Creepy.
Yes. You're the best detective in the world and both you and I know it. Nothing gets by you — I get it. But stop using the pedophile lines!

.

.

.

We all know, imperially, that Poirot was Agatha Christie's most clean and upright character. But goddamn if he doesn't sound like a total pedo sometimes!

.

.

.

.

.

.

.

.

.

.

.

.

.

.

Of course, the Dame of Crime wasn't the only one to fall prey to the unforgiving nature of modern minds and the depths they've fallen.

.

.

.

I give you Robert Lewis Stevenson, as specimen no.2.

Let me set the scene : our great protagonist, Doctor Jekyll, is describing the superior circumstances of his birth and station :

> I was born in the year 18— to a large fortune, endowed besides with excellent parts.
> — *Dr. Jekyll and Mr. Hyde*, Robert Lewis Stevenson

*snicker, excellent parts, you say ?

.

.

.

.

.

.

.

I suspect that because we have become more comfortable with the description of sexual acts, words we now use to describe the medical act of procreation, say *ejaculation*, are now so tightly linked with this act, that they can no longer be used in daily parlance without a giggle.

This was not always the case. Especially, in Victorian England, where they invented a new word, Rooster, so as to avoid using the word Cock in describing a male chicken. Or 'Drumstick' to not mention 'chicken thigh's'. Because mentioning a chicken's thigh inevitably leads the mind to think of other thigh's, which naturally leads one to the thought of the most delightful thigh's on the planet, the *female thigh*. So to avoid such a devastatingly sexually charged thought, let us rather militarize this lewd piece of chicken-meat, and call it the drumstick. [1]

**don't ask me why the chicken is so vulnerable to sexualization of terms. If you've ever seen one pecking about a dung heap, sex is the last thing on your mind.

.

.

.

ANYwho. I was saying—

So Doyle. Master of detective fiction. Before people were throwing about words like penis and vulva and masturbation, we hadn't relegating words like *ejaculation* to an exclusive description of the male sexual experience. Cannon balls could ejaculate from a shooting device, cream could be ejaculated from a doughnut, a rocket could prematurely ejaculate from it's launchpad—

.

.

.

I know I'm sounding a bit like I'm trying to find

nonsexual synonyms which are obviously sexual. But it was absolutely not on purpose! Do you see how loaded this term is??

Which makes it all the more funny that Sir Arthur Conan Doyle himself speaks of Sherlock Holmes ejaculating all over the place. *How did he not see this as hilariously dirty?*

And he doesn't just do this once or twice. He ejaculates so often and repeatedly that one can't help being impressed with his stamina. This most a-sexual of literary characters is nonetheless prolific in his finishes!

I'll (*of course*) share some of the good ones —

.

.

.

"Wonderful!" I ejaculated.

"Commonplace," said Holmes, though I thought from his expression that he was pleased at my evident surprise and admiration.

.

.

"So he sat as I dropped off to sleep, and so he sat when a sudden ejaculation caused me to wake up."

.

.

"Finally, he sprang down with an ejaculation of satisfaction."

.

.

"...he gave a little ejaculation of impatience, and continued to stare into the street."

.

.

(And my simple favorite)

"My dear Holmes!" I ejaculated.

.

.

.

But let us not assume this archaic and dirty-as-hell humor was from the English only. The Germans had a bit of a thing for racyness, and not so understated as their anglophone-cousins across the waters. Tell me Goethe isn't using Mephistopheles to describe Faust's magic-juice on Gretchin's... chest.

"...At first your passion rose and overflowed... you poured
it all into her bosom— and now the brook runs dry again.

Or his slightly more literary allusion to boobs, (a reference to Song of Solomon,)

Mephistopheles : "I've often envied you the pair of roes
<boobs> that feed among the lilies"

Okay. C'mon. I know I'm being a little fatuous in my analysis of some of the great works of the western canon. But if you can't find ~~lewd~~ humor in the most serious pillars of classic literature, well then you just gave up half the fun of reading the snobby classics.

----

1. I've no idea if this story or line of etymological development is accurate, but it rings true to Victorian sensibility, so let us rather assume it is true instead of getting tangled up in the historicity of facts.

CHAPTER 11

On to more serious topics—

    ·

    ·

    ·

    ·

    ·

    ·

    ·

<<on the question of *who* is directing the universe/life/existence.>>

    ·

The devil speaking
'—man, of course. Since there is no God.'

    ·

    ·

'...Permit me to ask you then, how can man be directing things, if he not only lacks the capacity to draw up any sort of plan for even a laughably short period of time, say even a thousand years.

... the man who just recently supposed he was directing

something turns out suddenly to be lying motionless in a wooden box.

...man is mortal, but that would still be just a minor problem. *The bad thing is that he's sometimes suddenly mortal, and that's the whole point!'*

.

.

.

.

.

.

.

.

.

.

... "do at least believe in the devil."

.

.

.

.

.

<<...long Russian exposition and conversation...>>

.

.

.

.

.

.

Master and Margarita, —Mikhail Bulgakov

CHAPTER 12

Gwendolyn : In matters of grave importance, style, not
sincerity, is the vital thing.
— *The Importance of being Earnest*, Oscar Wilde

THIS IS PRECISELY why I suggest we all take our most
serious life advice and coaching from Oscar Wilde.

And because this book is trying to be a bit of meta-
every-book, it is necessary for me to include a chapter of
deep philosophical investigation, from the greatest philoso-
pher of the modern age. No, not our modern philosophers
and psychologists ( ), or Descart, or Robespierre or Shake-
speare or Aquinas. Have you not been paying attention??
Oscar Wilde.

Of course, in keeping with the theme of this meta-book,
I've done you the favor of removing all the extras and will
keep this necessary life-advice to a few key quotations,
saving your time. And all the wisdom will be taken from a
single one of his plays[1], saving my time.

Again, you're welcome. And no. I will not apologize for optimizing my research and restricting us to one work.

.

.

.

.

ON MARRIAGE :
"The very essence of love is uncertainty. If I ever get married, I'll certainly try and forget the fact."

.

.

.

ON PROVIDING JUSTIFICATION :
"Produce your explanation, and pray make it improbable."

.

.

.

ON TRUTH :
"The truth is rarely pure, and never simple. Modern life would be rather tedious if it were either."

.

.

.

ON THE TRAGEDY OF LOSING ONES PARENTS :
"To lose one parent may be regarded as a misfortune; to lose both looks like carelessness."

.

.

ON BEAUTIFUL WOMEN :
"The only way to behave to a woman is to make love to her, if she is pretty, and to someone else, if she is plain."

.

.

.

ON GERMAN :

"I don't like German. It isn't at all a becoming language. I know perfectly well that I look quite plain after my German lesson."

Okay, I know that's not a particularly profound truth — but as the author of this anthology, I've a rather specific and personal criticism of German and have the executive decision, irrespective of my readership, to mark it a necessary wisdom for this chapter.

.

.

ON THE REAL REASON doctor Frankenstein shouldn't be raising people from the dead, even if one day such a doctor develops the capability :

"After we had all been resigned to his loss, his sudden return seems to me rather distressing."

.

.

.

ON FASTING :

"I never go without my dinner. No one ever does, except vegetarians and people like that."

.

.

.

ON THE IMPORTANCE OF GOOD LOOKS :

"He has nothing but looks everything. What more could one desire?"

.

. . .

Alright. Enough wisdom. But just to flesh this out, I'll go one step further. This isn't just the summarization of the most necessary life wisdom. I'm going to go schoolhouse on you and end with a few necessary and mind-probing cheesy questions. You know, to make sure you've internalized and thought about some of this stuff, workbook style.

Cheesy Questions :

Would you rather live in a country estate surrounded by far reaching lawns and forests, segregating you from the delights of society, *or* a ritzy penthouse down in the center of things? *Superficial and short sighted answers will be weighted higher.*

Both Jack and Algernon try to change their names to win the love of the women they adore. What's something ridiculous *you* did to win the love of someone you adored? *Be specific. Extra points for shameful details* :

If you were Dr. Jekyll, would you drink a mysterious potion that would remove the dark and evil parts of your personality? *Be honest!*

(You got me—wrong book. But think outside the box).

Use the bulleted lines on the rest of this and the following page to continue your essays.

-
-
-
-
-
-
-
-
-
-
-
-
-
-
-
-
-
-
-
-
-
-
-
-
-

 ·
 ·
 ·
 ·
 ·
 ·
 ·
 ·
 ·
 ·
 ·
 ·
 ·
 ·
 ·
 ·
 ·
 ·
 ·

---

1. The importance of Being Earnest. Obviously. I already quoted it at the top of the chapter! Pay attention!

CHAPTER 13

"I loved her. It was love at first sight. At last sight. At ever and ever sight." — *Lolita,* Vladimir Nabokov

INNOVATION IS the secret of writing a new story. Because there is no new story. It's all 'boy-meets-girl' and 'the-hero's-journey'. And usually both together. Or as Kurt Vonnegut said, (paraphrase), there are only three types of story (and their inverses) :

1 : Rags to Riches (and the inverse) - low start to ending high

2 : Man in a Hole (and the inverse) - A fall, then rise

3 : Cinderella (and inverse) - Rise, Fall, Rise.

All stories have been told because we've only so many ways of moving a story in a two-dimensional story world — namely up or down. So the question is, why are we still mesmerized by new stories and why do we act surprised when we get to the end of a really great book?

Answer: Innovation. Every romance has a 'boy meets girl' scene. Every thriller has a 'villain torturing the hero'. Every War story a battle scene. Every cowyboy-western a 'justice prevails' scene. It's the definition of story and the definition of the genres within that there are necessary structures and elements to not only story, but story in general.

Innovation is when these necessary parts are presented in a new and unique way. For example, in Lolita, the hero's journey is the story of a pedophile. The leading question of course always being, can Nabokov engender any sort of empathy for his lead when you're disgusted by his character.

Whether he can or can't is beside the point. But there's a certain dark wisdom to the story he writes, which he's able to explore because he turns the convention of hero upside down. The truth of how, if you leave the naturally occurring urges and desires of man free rein, without any attempt at a moral limit, he will destroy himself. That it doesn't matter what paradigm of morality you create to justify your actions, the ultimate rules of the universe are unassailable: you do evil, and evil will destroy you.

We can debate about whether or not *ultimate-good* actually exists, but no one who actually sees the world questions the existence of the devil.

.

.

.

.

.

.

"Untroubled, scornful, outrageous — that is how wisdom wants us to be: she is a woman and never loves anyone but a warrior."

— *Thus Spoke Zarathustra,* Friedrich Nietzsche

CHAPTER 14

I PROMISED you a Dostoyevsky-style random essay in the middle of this.

Well, okay. It's not Dostoyevsky-level. The topic is pretty benign. But in the spirit of dropping an essay in the middle of a story, here it goes —

IN DEFENSE OF THE SEXUALIZATION OF THE BREAST

There is a movement afoot, in case you've been living under a *very* large and internet proof rock, to reclaim the breast. 'Breasts are for milk,' women chant in breastfeeding sit-ins at cafés and on street corners.

Legally, in most western countries to my knowledge, women are allowed to breast feed anywhere they are otherwise allowed to be. But the battle they fight is now not with legislation and courts, but with the sexualization of the breast. This, they argue, has created a public stigma against a woman breastfeeding without a cover. Why is it, they demand, that most people don't bat an eye when a woman wears a high-exposure top that reveals much more than the typical breastfeeding mum. Why may a woman wear booty shorts with the cheeks of her bum hanging out, and a top so low you can see the bow on her brasier, yet pop a suckling baby on a breast, and all of a sudden you get looks of disgust and annoyance? Breast are, first and foremost, tools for feeding ones offspring, they argue. Take back the breast!

And I get it. Breasts are not just a sexual object, but are a highly functioning tool in a woman's arsenal for the care of her children. In the scheme of procreation, a woman might well use her breasts longer than she uses her uterus.

But.

But in our defense of a woman's right to breastfeed comfortably without the ogling stares of sexually deprived men and the glares of shopkeeps concerned with their patronage, I would like to point something out. *Breasts are also sexual.* And I think that's ok. I even *gasp* like that they are.

Perhaps this essay could only be written by a woman - a man might get crucified for admitting that he likes that breasts are sex symbols. And then, only a woman who has used her breasts not just as objects of sexual attraction but also as a mother who has already breastfed for many years. I've used my twins on both fronts, so I consider myself sufficiently experienced to make this defense.

Motherhood is astounding. The capacity of a woman's body to create another human is something quite incredible.

And then, once that human being is created, to be able to nourish it from ones own body with the perfectly crafted and nutritious nectar that breast milk is — breathtaking. Truly breathtaking.

But you know what is sometimes a trial as a mother? Retaining ones sense of sexuality. Of being something more than just a milk machine and waste management worker. That breasts are useful tools should not be minimized, of course. But that they can be objects of beauty and sexuality is also a legitimate aspect of their province. Life is meant not to be only functional, but also beautiful. I would posit that often when a young mother becomes depressed, it is partly because they've lost a sense of their own function as creatures of beauty and individuals in their own right and see life now as a series of functions. But life is more than functional. It should be lived with energy and excitement and love and even lust. We should treasure our bodies as not just tools, but also appreciate the aspects of our lives that make life exciting. Lust and desire, love and passion, relationships and beauty.

It is from this place of seeing a woman body as only a tool that women stage nurse-ins and demand the freedom to nurse without shame in public places.

But let me defend the other side. That in our current society, breasts can also sexualized. *And that is ok.* Because sexuality is also a legitimate aspect - even if there isn't really any clear reason *why* breasts specifically are sexual.

A century and a half ago, ankles were considered sexually charged. That a man should see or *shudder* touch a woman's ankle was considered highly invasive of a woman's propriety.

Ankles, I would argue, have an even higher function than breasts, and a much less clear explanation as to why they should be objects of sexual attraction. (Although I do see how a well formed ankle is the necessity of a beautiful leg.)

My point is, however, that what we see as sexual changes over time, somewhat inexplicably. Why a breast or an ankle or a bum is an object of sexual attention may be somewhat arbitrary. But we should enjoy that we can have these symbols of sexuality just as we should appreciate that we have rotating ankles that play such a necessary role in our mobility and breasts that can nourish our children for the first months of life.

The iPod was not a roaring success just because it was a good mp3 player - we'd had many mp3 players before it came on the market. But it was a brilliant success because it was a sexy mp3 player. The design was so pleasing. The device was not only simple to use, but fun to play with! *smirk

The irony is not lost on me that early waves of feminism fought to defend women against the idea that they were mere objects. They argued that women were not just tools for mens sexual appetites and a man's need to sire children. They were also complex beings in their own right, aside from the value a man put on them. This argument that breasts should only be seen as functional objects and not also simply beautiful in their own right — brings us full circle. If a woman is more than just a baby maker, then her body should be more than just function.

All this is to say that there is an argument to be made for covering up when breast feeding. As women and mothers, let us preserve our sexuality. Women are not just functional tools to an end, but also beautiful ideas. If we push this too hard, that one should be able to breastfeed anywhere because eating is a necessary part of an infants life, we run the risk of destroying an aspect of sexuality that is as much a true part of our bodies as is the function.

Let's not go there. Don't take the beauty and passion out of life.

"You're given the form, but you have to write the sonnet yourself." — *A Wrinkle in Time, Madeleine l'Engle*

.

.

.

Life is like a limerick.

I know we just saw that life is a Sonnet, but that's asking a lot. When we get to live 300+ years we can say it's a sonnet. But for the moment, we're still living Limerick lengths, so let's just be honest about it.

Life gives us a strictly defined structure and form. You don't get to break the fundamental rules. But within those bounds anything could be said or done[1].

.

.

.

.

Life :

__ __ __ __ __ __ __ __ __ (A)

__ __ __ __ __ __ __ __ (A)

__ __ __ __ __ (B)

__ __ __ __ __ __ (B)

__ __ __ __ __ __ __ __ __ (A)

.

.

.

Go ahead. Play around with it. See what you can come up with

up with

.

.

.

.

.

.

.

.

.

.

By way of concrete example :

Life of Bobby

There once was a young lad named Bobby.
Who read books as some odd sort of hobby.
The greats he didn't know,
Though he swore t'werent so.
And that's why we all t'ink he's snobby.
— Anon.[2]

.

.

.

.

.

.

.

.

.

.

.

.

.

.

.

.

.

.

.

.

.

.

.

.

The End

---

1. The parallels don't end with structure. As Wikipedia says, "the form is essentially transgressive; violation of taboo is part of its function." — *smirk.
2. Of course, if footnote #1 is true, (and some say it is indeed *not*), — then my example of a limerick isn't technically accurate, being as it is in no way transgressive or a violation of taboo. Unless of course, you would say that claiming that the leader of the 'Snobby Classics Book Club" hasn't read the classics is a rather taboo sort of thing to claim—in which case : done.

HUMANS ARE the most complicated objects on earth, and until we find extraterrestrial life forms, the most interesting objects in the universe. The layers of complexity only become more mind boggling the more we understand them. From the individual cells that operate still largely beyond our understanding, (despite being the focused subject of study for many decades), to the forces that motivate and confound us on a group level, and every level or resolution in-between. The ideas we create, the systems we are part of, the ability for the consciousness we harbor to be self-reflective — it is all so complicated that we still have no consensus on the fundamental nature of any of those levels.

What motivates humans? A search for happiness and well being, or a need for purpose and meaning? What is consciousness? What is life? What is the fundamental nature of the matter and energy of which we're formed— and does that nature form or affect our consciousness? What is the proper way to operate in the social community?

All these most fundamental questions are still being discussed because there is no consensus. Some individuals might have decided for themselves some of these higher level questions (the philosophy ones), but the fact that it's not at all broadly agreed on means there is enough uncertainty that the questions have not been settled. And that's just the small stuff.

Story is the medium I find most useful to explore these broader-level questions. There are minds brighter than mine trying to figure out the science and nature of reality, but the more complicated questions about how to live rightly in the world, how we should conduct ourselves as part of the group, and what the meaning of existence is— these are questions we understand in story. These are the questions that still need to be acted out in a symbolic manner (story).

I believe this is also why humans are so obsessed with stories. Our very nature seeks to understand the world around us, and since we became conscious, we have been using this medium to explain and describe how our world works. This is why the romance story (how to act in a social world) and the hero's journey (how to face the unknown, enter the world of the extraordinary to find your gift and return to the ordinary to share your knowledge) are the two most fundamental stories of all time — which despite all the stories that we've been told and have seen, continue to lock us in attention.

Why bother with the snobby classics? Because these are the stories that tap into the nature of our human story most archetypically.

Usually. It is also the case that a book can enter the canon because it did a thing first. But, meh. They're usually not the fun ones to read.

At the time of this writing, I was living in Munich. If this book survives long enough, hopefully that information will become outdated.

I do sometimes take time from my normal writing pursuits to create random books like this. But I am most interested in exploring the good vs. evil stories that play out in crime fiction.

My first book, *The Year of the Rabid Dragon,* was a medical mystery about an engineered virus that is released into Beijing. I realize that was a bit on the nose speaking now in 2020, but it was published two years before COVID-19 broke. That story is as much a glimpse at the people that make up Beijing and a social and political world so different from North America and Western Europe as it is the crime that shape the plot.

I love hearing from readers. Look me up on the major social media platforms (mostly @lhdraken) or email me directly at

lh@lhdraken.com.

To continue hearing more of my ramblings, join my mailing list at :

www.lhdraken.com

But most of call, keep reading, and never stop asking *why*.

NOTES

NOTES

NOTES

www.ingramcontent.com/pod-product-compliance
Lightning Source LLC
Chambersburg PA
CBHW021704110726
47902CB00007B/2063